SNOW WHITE

AND THE SEVEN DWARFS

Retold by Kay Brown
Illustrated by Gerry Embleton

Long, long ago in a far off land, a young Queen gave birth to a pretty dark-haired daughter. The King and Queen named her Snow White, because she was born on a beautiful wintry day.

However, when Snow White was still a little girl her mother died — and the King was very lonely.

Soon he married again, but his new wife was a cold and cruel woman. She was also strangely beautiful and spent many hours alone in a high tower room admiring herself in the mirror.

She shouted at the servants, snapped at Snow White and never smiled at the poor, kind King. It was whispered in the castle that she had cast a spell on him to *make* him choose her for his new Queen... and they were right! For she was a wicked witch, with a shrivelled heart full of dark and evil secrets.

Year by year Snow White grew more gentle and loving — and more beautiful — and the King spent most of his days with his sweet little daughter, for then they were both happy. Watching them together the wicked Queen's jealousy of Snowwhite turned to hatred.

She spent more and more time alone in her tower room, practicing terrible and spiteful spells. Each day she would stare admiringly at herself in the magic mirror, asking:

Mirror, mirror, tell me do
Am I the fairest? Now tell me true!

Imagine her fury when, one day, the mirror replied:

You *were* the fairest, it is true,
But Snow White is lovelier now than you!

In a jealous rage she hurled her goblet at the wall!

No one would challenge her beauty — Snow White must die!

The wicked Queen summoned a woodcutter
who lived nearby in the forest and ordered him
to take Snow White deep into the wood and
kill her.
The woodcutter was a kind man, however, and didn't
like the new Queen. Next day he and Snow White set
off for a walk. By evening they had reached the thickest
part of the forest and Snow White was very tired. While
she slept, the woodcutter crept away, leaving her
unharmed.

When Snow White awoke to find herself alone and in a
strange place she was very frightened. Trying to find a
path, she wandered wearily until it was dark. Suddenly,
near to tears, she saw a light through the trees! In a
few minutes she was in front of a fat little cottage,
quite unlike anything she had ever seen. She walked in.

Inside the cottage it was warm and comfortable.
Snow White explored the many rooms, hardly noticing
how small they were. At last she found what she had
been looking for — a big, soft bed! She was much too
tired to notice the seven fat pillows, the seven thick,
white blankets and the seven empty mugs beside the
bed. She stretched out, yawned... and fell into a deep,
untroubled sleep.

What Snowwhite didn't know was that the little house
belonged to seven strong dwarfs, who had built it
themselves. Each dwarf had a long, white beard (of
which he was very proud) and, because they all looked
rather alike each wore a different coloured cap.

They worked all day in their mines far beneath the earth, carving the rock in their search for gold, silver and crystal — and for the sheer dwarfish love of mining and cutting the stones!

Having done their day's work (dwarfs start
very early and finish after dark) they
returned home over the hill.

The sound of their merry chattering woke
Snow White, who thought for a moment she
must still be dreaming when she saw the
seven puzzled little men staring at her!

She started to explain how she came to be
in the cottage and, finding the dwarfs so
kind and understanding, gradually told them
the whole story — about her dear father,
her unkind stepmother and the woodcutter.
She became very upset and, when the dwarfs
asked her to live with them in safety she
gladly agreed.

Snow White stayed with her new friends
and was very happy. She grew to love them all for
although they were rough, they were always kind. They
took her often to the ancient dwarf mines and showed
her the halls of shining crystal and the caves and lakes
far beneath the hill. Snow White's days were busy,
keeping the cottage bright and neat, cooking for the
little men and washing their colourful clothes — seven
of everything and fourteen tiny stockings! — and her
beauty and gaiety filled their lives with joy.

Beyond the forest the witch, locked in her room
in the castle, again asked her mirror:
    Mirror, mirror, tell me do
    Now who is the fairest? Tell me do!
Unbelievably, the mirror replied:
    Snow White is fairer still than you:
    Deep in the forest by their mines
    With kindly dwarfs, good friends and true,
    Her laughter rings, her beauty shines!

Hearing this the wicked Queen screamed with rage and swore Snow White would not escape again! Having sent her nasty pet crow to find out where Snow White was hiding, she cast a spell and changed herself into a fat old pedlar woman. On top of the trinkets in her basket she placed a comb which she had dipped in a deadly poison and, when the crow returned, she set off eagerly to the dwarfs' house.

Snow White was busy cleaning the tiny cottage windows when she saw the pedlar woman. She ran to the gate and took the pretty comb. As soon as it touched her head she fell down... unconscious! Muttering contentedly to herself, the witch hurried away.

Luckily, however, the dwarfs had decided to stop work early that day to take Snow White for a picnic. When they arrived home they found her lying by the gate, the comb in her hand. Remembering her stories of the jealous stepmother they threw the comb far into the trees — and as soon as it had disappeared Snow White recovered.

Immediately the Queen reached the castle she asked her mirror the usual question and was told once more that Snow White's beauty was greater than hers! Even angrier now that she had failed again, the witch turned herself into a different old woman and left to find Snow White once more.

Now although the dwarfs had warned Snow White about speaking to strangers, she was so pleased to see a new face that she allowed the witch into the cottage. As she tried a new velvet bodice, the wicked witch offered to tighten the laces... and pulled them so tight that Snow White fainted!

This time the dwarfs arrived home only just in time to save her, by cutting the laces. They were very cross that Snow White had ignored their advice about strangers and warned her very sternly not to be so foolish again!

Back at the castle, and sure of her success this time, the witch was horrified to learn from the mirror that Snow White was still alive. From her oldest and most evil book of spells she brewed a powerful poison, with which she filled a rosy apple.

Changing her appearance yet again —
this time she became a cackling country
woman — she set off as if to market.
Passing the dwarfs' house she pretended
to have lost her way and called to
Snow White for directions. At first
Snow White, remembering what the dwarfs
had said, refused to help — but the old
woman pleaded for so long that,
trustingly, Snow White agreed to direct her
from the window... and
was given the apple in thanks.
She took only one bite
          and fell down
                    quite dead.

As the witch turned to leave, the seven dwarfs appeared over the hill. When they realised what had happened their anger was truly frightening — and dwarfs are not easily affected by magic! The witch fled for her life through the trees and up the rocky mountains. Whether she was lost, or killed by the wild storms, or whether she escaped by some remembered spell we shall never know. What is certain is that she has *never* ever returned to that forest or any part of the King's country again.

Utterly broken-hearted, the dwarfs tried in vain to bring Snow White back to life. How empty the little house seemed without her smiling face and how quiet without her laughter. With tears in their eyes they worked all night, carving a coffin of the finest crystal from the heart of the mountain. Gently they placed Snow White inside and carried it to a nearby hill. There they stood guard over it in sad silence — hoping that one day some passer-by might be able to break the spell...

Almost a year passed while
Snow White lay still and cold
in the crystal coffin, watched
over by her faithful friends.
At last a young prince, troubled by
dreams of a beautiful, dark-haired girl
imprisoned in crystal, came seeking
her. Seeing the face from his dreams
he was overcome with love for her and
gently kissed her lips.
The spell was broken! — with a sharp
crack the coffin
shattered and
Snow White
awoke.

Seeing the color return to Snow White's cheeks
as she walked hand-in-hand with her prince, the dwarfs
danced and hugged each other for joy. It was plain that
a different kind of magic had filled both their hearts
with love.

Snow White and the prince delighted in each other's
company and their love and happiness grew day by
day. Soon they were married and in time they, too, had
a pretty, dark-haired daughter — whom they called
Snow White.